W9-AVK-449

THE DARK KNIGHT RISES™

HarperFestival is an imprint of HarperCollins Publishers.

The Dark Knight Rises: I Am Bane
Copyright © 2012 DC Comics.
BATMAN and all related characters and elements
are trademarks of and © DC Comics.
(s12)

HARP5005
Printed in the United States of America. No part of this
book may be used or reproduced in any manner whatsoever
without written permission except in the case of brief
quotations embodied in critical articles and reviews.
For information address HarperCollins Children's Books,
a division of HarperCollins Publishers,
10 East 53rd Street, New York, NY 10022.
www.harpercollinschildrens.com

Library of Congress catalog card number: 2011945725
ISBN 978-0-06-213222-2

Book design by John Sazaklis

12 13 14 15 16 CWM 10 9 8 7 6 5 4 3 2 1
❖
First Edition

THE DARK KNIGHT RISES™

I Am Bane

ADAPTED BY LUCY ROSEN

DIGITAL ART BY SCOTT COHN

INSPIRED BY THE FILM
THE DARK KNIGHT RISES

SCREENPLAY BY
JONATHAN NOLAN AND
CHRISTOPHER NOLAN

STORY BY
CHRISTOPHER NOLAN
AND **DAVID S. GOYER**

BATMAN CREATED BY
BOB KANE

HARPER FESTIVAL
An Imprint of HarperCollinsPublishers

Inside the Gotham City Stock Exchange, a janitor stopped mopping the floor to scan the crowded lobby. Busy people hustled in and out of the elevators. Security guards kept close watch on the doors. Off to the side, two shoe shiners were tending customers.

It seemed like any other day in this important building. But things were about to change.

"Everybody down!" yelled the janitor, throwing his mop to the ground. The shoe shiners jerked up immediately and pulled black masks over their faces. Some of the security guards jumped out from behind the desk in full combat gear.

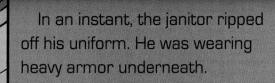

In an instant, the janitor ripped off his uniform. He was wearing heavy armor underneath.

"Listen up," cried the mysterious villain. "I am Bane, and you are at my mercy. I'm not leaving here until I get what I want." He glared at the terrified crowd in front of him, then pointed to his henchmen. "Get to work," he snarled.

Bane's goons stormed the lobby, knocking people down and clearing Bane's way. Bane grabbed the head security officer by the shirt. "Give me access to the computer," he threatened, "or I'll tear this place apart."

Trembling, the officer handed over the keys to the computer vault. Bane tossed him aside like a dishrag. As Bane tore open the door to the vault, the guard crept slowly to his desk. He pressed a tiny red button beneath the counter without anyone seeing.

The button set off two alarms—one in Gotham's police station, the other far beneath Wayne Manor. Bruce Wayne's underground chamber was the center of operations for his secret life. He was Batman!

"Something's happening at the stock exchange," Bruce told his butler, Alfred. "There's no time to lose."

Bruce put on the Batsuit. Alfred handed him a special new weapon. "You might need this, sir," he said.

"Thanks," said Bruce as he roared out of the Batcave in the Bat-Pod. Batman was on his way!

At the stock exchange, things were going from bad to worse. The police were on the scene, but they were no match for Bane's army of goons.

In the computer vault, Bane pulled out some electronic equipment from his bag. He plugged it into the stock exchange's computer, which stored all of Gotham City's financial records.

Bane laughed as he downloaded bank account numbers, security codes, and personal records from Gotham's citizens. "The days of the rich ruling this city are over," he boomed. Without money or control over the city's resources, the citizens of Gotham didn't stand a chance against Bane.

Bane burst out of the computer vault and barreled through the lobby. "Mission accomplished," he yelled at his henchmen. "Let's move!"

In a flash, the villainous group was tearing down the streets of Gotham on high-powered motorcycles. Bane's computer gear was safely secured. He was going to get away!

Bane spotted a dark figure in the distance. The figure was getting closer and closer, faster and faster. It was Batman! The Dark Knight was on the Bat-Pod, careening toward the villains. He was not slowing down!

At the last second, Batman swerved to the side. He used the weapon Alfred gave him to blast the motorcycles Bane's henchmen were riding. ZAP! The weapon let out a strong electromagnetic pulse, draining the bikes of all of their power.

As the motorcycles sputtered and skidded down the street, the bad guys flew up into the air and came crashing down in front of the Bat-Pod. Batman jumped off and knocked each one out cold, tying them up against a streetlight.

Bane was getting away! "Your turn," growled Batman. He roared down the street on the Bat-Pod, doing everything he could to catch the evil mastermind. But Bane was still going strong.

Batman shot a Batarang at Bane's motorcycle. The sharp metal tore right through the tires, sending Bane tumbling along the pavement. He let go of the bag with the downloaded information. "No!" cried Bane, reaching for the bag. But Batman grabbed it.

"You're not going to rule this city," Batman snarled, tying Bane up. "Not on my watch."

Batman brought Bane over to where the other criminals were trapped. The police had just arrived. "I don't know how we can thank you," said Police Commissioner Gordon.

Gordon didn't even have a chance to try. When he turned around to face Batman, the Dark Knight was already gone.